811 Francis, R
        Like ghosts of
eagles
                            750

FEB 1 1 1975

LIKE GHOSTS OF EAGLES

Like Ghosts of Eagles: Poems

DRAWINGS BY JACK COUGHLIN

1966-1974 by Robert Francis

UNIVERSITY OF MASSACHUSETTS PRESS

Line 1 of the poem "Cats" is quoted
from Olaus Murie, *Field Guide to
Animal Tracks,*
The Peterson Field Guide Series
(Boston: Houghton Mifflin Co.,
1954), p. 113

Thanks go to the following for the
courtesy of copyright assignment:

The Virginia Quarterly Review,
United Church Herald, Quabbin,
New Poems by American Poets
(1953), The Massachusetts Review,
The Lyric, Field, Commonweal,
Colloquy.

"The Mountain" and "Suspension"
first appeared in *The New-England
Galaxy.*

"Peacock," "The Righteous,"
"Exemplary," "Prescription," and
"A Fear" first appeared in *The
Land on the Tip of a Hair,* poems
in wood carved by Wang Hui-Ming.

"Blood Stains," "A Health to
Earth," "Silent Poem," "Going to
the Funeral," "On a Theme by
Frost," and "Cats" were published
as a portfolio, *Six Poems,* with four
accompanying etchings by Jack
Coughlin.

"Chimàphila, 1972," "Three Old
Ladies and Three Spring Bulbs,"
and "November" first appeared in
the Winter 1974 issue of *A Review,*
Amherst College, copyright ©
1974 by A Review.

"Blue Cornucopia" first appeared in
the Spring 1974 issue of *The New-
England Galaxy,* copyright © 1974
by Old Sturbridge Inc.

FOR L. S.

*Whose constant expectation
of poems has helped significantly
to bring those poems into being.*

Contents

One

The Mountain

does not move the mountain is not moved
it rises yet in rising rests and there
are moments when its unimaginable weight
is weightless as a cloud it does not come
to me nor do I need to go to it I only
need that it should be should loom always
the mountain is and I am I and now a cloud
like a white butterfly above a flower.

Like Ghosts of Eagles

The Indians have mostly gone
but not before they named the rivers
the rivers flow on
and the names of the rivers flow with them
    Susquehanna   Shenandoah

The rivers are now polluted plundered
but not the names of the rivers
cool and inviolate as ever
pure as on the morning of creation
    Tennessee   Tombigbee

If the rivers themselves should ever perish
I think the names will somehow somewhere hover
like ghosts of eagles
those mighty whisperers
    Missouri   Mississippi.

4

A Health to Earth

and her magnificent digestion
like a great cow she chews her cud
nothing defeats her   nothing escapes

the owl ejects an indigestible
pellet   earth ejects nothing
she who can masticate a mountain

what is a little junk to her
a little scrap   like a great cow
she chews it over   she takes her time

all man's perdurable fabrications
his structural steel, his factories, forts
his moon machines   she will in time

like a great summer-pasture cow
digest   in time assimilate
it all to pure geology.

Chimàphila, 1972

How easily I could have missed you
Your quiet blooming those July days
Noisy with the Democratic Convention

And all the other noises. All flowers
Are silent but some more so than others
And none more silent than Chimàphila

Whose petals are not sun-white daisy-white
But the subdued glow of forests
Dim with their dimness, a nodding flower.

A hundred blossoms and more I counted
Gathered in Quaker meeting, a hundred
Where in former years perhaps a dozen.

For you a late spring and a rainy summer
Must rate as blessing. How otherwise
Should Nineteen Seventy-two have been so banner?

Chimàphila, the winter-loving (so the Greek)
But oh how summer-loving when the still air
Lingers and broods over your intense sweetness.

6

Clearly whatever my woodland soil offers
Is all you ask, you of all flowers.
So I can say that you return my love.

Long after your petals fall and your fragrance
Is only in my mind, after deep snow
I will call up again and again your name.

Overhearing Two on
a Cold Sunday Morning

We left our husbands sleeping,
Sun in our eyes and the cold air
Calling us out, yet not too cold
For winter to be rehearsing spring
At ten o'clock in the morning.

Like harps the telephone poles hum
And the glass insulators dazzle.
We left them warm in bed dreaming
Of primavera, dreaming no doubt
Of fountains, fauns, and dolphins.

Chickadees dance on the wind. They
Are young, our husbands, especially
As they lie sleeping. Sometimes
We imagine we are older than they
Though actually we're a little younger.

We have come up into the upper light.
We have come out into the outer air.
We could almost for a moment forget
Our husbands. No, that is not true.
Never for a moment can we forget them.

Soon we will go back to them and shout
"This is a beautiful day!" Or if
They are still sleeping, whisper it
Into their ears or on their lips.
We do not often leave them sleeping.

Prayer to A.N.W.
(Presuming on his name)

O towering peak O venerable pate
O snowfall beard O berg O bard
Send us your storms your Sturm-und-Drang
Let all your rhymes be winter rime
And smite and bless us with your wrath
O king philosopher-king O Alfred
Teach us to love the overwhelming
Then lull us lull us to sleep at last
Like infants cradled in the blast.

10

Silent Poem

backroad leafmold stonewall chipmunk
underbrush grapevine woodchuck shadblow

woodsmoke cowbarn honeysuckle woodpile
sawhorse bucksaw outhouse wellsweep

backdoor flagstone bulkhead buttermilk
candlestick ragrug firedog brownbread

hilltop outcrop cowbell buttercup
whetstone thunderstorm pitchfork steeplebush

gristmill millstone cornmeal waterwheel
watercress buckwheat firefly jewelweed

gravestone groundpine windbreak bedrock
weathercock snowfall starlight cockcrow

Blue Cornucopia

Pick any blue   sky-blue   cerulean   azure
cornflower   periwinkle   blue-eyed grass
blue bowl   bluebell   pick lapis lazuli
blue pool   blue girl   blue Chinese vase
or pink-blue chicory alias ragged sailor
or sapphire   bluebottle fly   indigo bunting
blue dragonfly or devil's darning needle
blue-green   turquoise   peacock   blue spruce
blue verging on violet   the fringed gentian
gray-blue   blue bonfire smoke   autumnal
haze   blue hill   blueberry   distance
and darker blue   storm-blue   blue goose
ink   ocean   ultramarine   pick winter
blue snow-shadows   ice   the blue star Vega.

November

Ruin of summer, wrecker of gardens,
A stingy sun, interminable rain—
Indicted, hailed into court, what do you say?

Balm for tired eyes my umber and grey embers,
My interlude between two brilliancies.
Time now for fireplace to grant the fire.

But in the woods, look, jewel-green my moss
And on each branch the strung beads of small buds
Ready for winter and for beyond winter.

December

Dim afternoon December afternoon
Just before dark, their caps
A Christmas or un-Christmas red
The hunters.

Oh, I tell myself that death
In the woods is far far better
Than doom in the slaughterhouse.
Still, the hunters haunt me.

Does a deer die now or does a hunter
Dim afternoon December afternoon
By cold intent or accident but always
My death?

Two

History

I

History to the historian
Is always his story.

He puts the pieces
Of the past together

To make his picture
To make his peace—

Pieces of past wars
Pieces of past peaces.

But don't ask him
To put the pieces

Of the past together
To make your picture

To make your peace.

II

The Holy See is not by any means
the whole sea and the whole sea
so far as one can see is far from holy.

The Holy See is old but how much older
the sea that is not holy, how vastly
older the sea itself, the whole sea.

The Holy See may last a long time longer
yet how much longer, how vastly longer
the whole sea, the sea itself, the unholy sea

Scrubbing earth's unecclesiastical shores
as if they never never would be clean
like a row of Irish washerwomen

Washing, washing, washing away
far into the unforeseeable future
long after the Holy See no more is seen.

III

Henry Thoreau Henry James and Henry Adams
would never have called history bunk
not Henry James not Henry Adams.

Nor would Henry Adams or Henry James
ever have tried to get the boys
out of the trenches by Christmas.

Only Henry Thoreau might have tried
to get the boys out of the bunk out
of the Christmas out of the trenches.

For Henry Thoreau was anti-bunk Henry James
pro-bunk and what shall we say of Henry Adams
except that all four Henrys are now history?

IV

The great Eliot has come the great Eliot
has gone and where precisely are we now?

He moved from the Mississippi to the Thames
and we moved with him a few miles or inches.

He taught us what to read what not to read
and when he changed his mind he let us know.

He coughed discreetly and we likewise coughed;
we waited and we heard him clear his throat.

How to be perfect prisoners of the past
this was the thing but now he too is past.

Shall we go sit beside the Mississippi
and watch the riffraft driftwood floating by?

On a Theme by Frost

Amherst never had a witch
Of Coòs or of Grafton

But once upon a time
There were three old women.

One wore a small beard
And carried a big umbrella.

One stood in the middle
Of the road hailing cars.

One drove an old cart
All over town collecting junk.

They were not weird sisters,
No relation to one another.

A duly accredited witch I
Never heard Amherst ever had

But as I say there
Were these three old women.

One was prone to appear
At the door (not mine!) :

"I've got my nightgown on,
I can stay all night."

One went to a party
At the president's house once

Locked herself in the bathroom
And gave herself a bath.

One had taught Latin, having
Learned it at Mount Holyoke.

Of course Amherst may have
Had witches I never knew.

The Bulldozer

Bulls by day
And dozes by night.

Would that the bulldozer
Dozed all the time

Would that the bulldozer
Would rust in peace.

His watchword
Let not a witch live

His battle cry
Better dead than red.

Give me the bullfinch
Give me the bulbul

Give me if you must
The bull himself

But not the bulldozer
No, not the bulldozer.

Cats

Cats walk neatly
Whatever they pick
To walk upon

Clipped lawn, cool
Stone, waxed floor
Or delicate dust

On feather snow
With what disdain
Lifting a paw

On horizontal glass
No less or
Ice nicely debatable

Wall-to-wall
Carpet, plush divan
Or picket fence

In deep jungle
Grass where we
Can't see them

Where we can't
Often follow follow
Cats walk neatly.

Trade

The little man with the long nose
and the camera around his neck
has corn in his pocket for the pigeons
    not that he loves them.

The little man with the long nose
will put a little corn in your hand
for the pigeons if you will let him
    not that he loves you.

The pigeons will come and cluster
about your hand flapping and fanning
and feeding till not a kernel is left
    not that they love you.

And the little man with the long nose
will take your picture and you will
put a little something in his hand
    not that you love him either.

The Peacock

The over-ornate can be a burden as peacock
proves the weight of whose preposterous plumes
is psychological see how his peacock back is bent
hysterical he stamps his foot one more pavane
and I will scream he screams spreading once more
for the ten thousandth time that fantastic fan.

Picasso and Matisse
(circa 1950)

At Vallauris and Vence, Picasso and Matisse,
A trifling eighteen miles apart,
Each with his chapel, one to God and one to Peace,
Artfully pursue their art.

What seems, not always is, what is, not always seems,
Not always what is so is such.
The Party and the Church at absolute extremes
Are nearly near enough to touch.

At Vallauris and Vence, Picasso and Matisse,
One old, one older than before,
Each with his chapel, one to God and one to Peace,
Peacefully pursue their war.

The Two Lords of Amherst

The two Lords, Jeffery and Jehovah, side by side
Proclaim that hospitality lives and Jesus died.

Jeffery in whitewashed brick, Jehovah in gray stone
Both testify man does not live by bread alone.

From sacred love to bed and board and love profane
One could dart back and forth and not get wet in rain.

How providentially inclusive the design:
Here are the cocktails, here the sacramental wine.

Here is the holy, here the not-so-holy host.
Here are the potted palms and here the Holy Ghost.

Tell, if you can and will, which is more richly blest:
The guest Jehovah entertains or Jeffery's guest.

The Pope

The Pope in Rome
Under St. Peter's dome
Is the Pope at home.

Pomp is his daily fare
Poised in his papal chair
Quite debonair.

The great bell peeling,
The cardinals kneeling,
The soaring ceiling—

All that display
Does not dismay
The Pope a single day.

Three

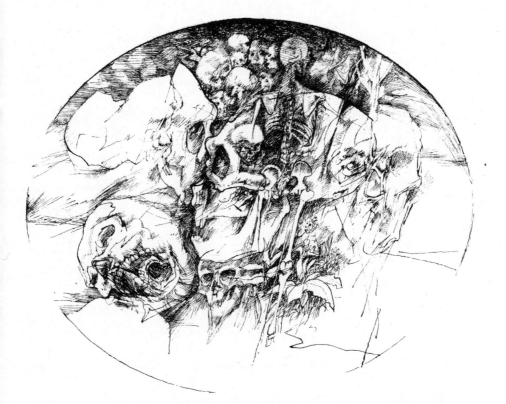

Light Casualties

Light things falling—I think of rain,
Sprinkle of rain, a little shower
And later the even lighter snow.

Falling and light—white petal-fall
Apple and pear, and then the leaves.
Nothing is lighter than a falling leaf.

Did the guns whisper when they spoke
That day? Did death tiptoe his business?
And afterwards in another world

Did mourners put on light mourning,
Casual as rain, as snow, as leaves?
Did a few tears fall?

The Righteous

After the saturation bombing divine
worship after the fragmentation shells
the organ prelude the robed choir after
defoliation Easter morning the white
gloves the white lilies after the napalm
Father Son and Holy Ghost Amen.

Blood Stains

blood stains   how to remove   from cotton
silk   from all fine fabrics   blood stains
where did I read   all I remember old stains
harder than fresh   old stains often indelible

blood stains   what did it say   from glass
shattered   from metal   memorial marble
how to remove   a clean soft cloth   was it
and plenty of tepid water   also from paper

headlines   dispatches   communiqués   history
white leaves   green leaves   from grass growing
or dead   from trees   from flowers   from sky
from standing from running water   blood stains

City

In the scare
city
no scarcity
of fear
of fire
no scarcity
of goons
of guns
in the scare
city
the scar
city

After the celebrated carved misericords
And various tombs, the amiable sexton
Shows you by St. Mary's door the stone
Where Cromwell's men sharpened their swords.

Was it not a just, a righteous, war
When indiscriminate Irish blood
Flowed for the greater glory of God
Outside St. Mary's door?

If righteousness be often tipped with steel,
Be rightly tipped, psalm-singing men
Will help themselves to holy stone
To whet their zeal.

So you have both: the mellow misericords
Gracing the choir
And just outside the door
The swords.

Epitaphs

THE PROUD AND PASSIONATE MAN

Stiff both in passion and in pride
He culminated when he died.

FISHERMAN

Now comes the fisherman to terms
Who erstwhile worked his will on worms.

THE FURRED LADY

What can this careful lady think
Who always wore in winter mink
Here on a day as cold as doom
To leave her mink wrap in her room?

BUTCHER

Falleth the rain, falleth the leaf,
The butcher now is one with beef.

EVERYMAN

Preacher or lecher, saint or sot,
What he was once he now is not.

UNDERTAKER

The man who yesterday was seen
On death to fatten on death grows lean.

TOMB OF A WELL-KNOWN SOLDIER

Here lies the military mind,
Alas, not all of it there is,
Though while he lived he was inclined
To act as though it all were his.

PREACHER

He called on God to smite the foe.
Missing his aim, God laid him low.

OLD LADY PATRIOT

How calm she lies in death, how calm
This one-time champion of the Bomb.

DIPLOMAT

Here lies a diplomat, alas,
Brought to one more complete impasse.

A Fear

Against a falling snow
I heard him long ago

A young man who could prove
Old Goethe could not love

Old love he both denied
And equally decried.

If I were young and cold
I'd be afraid to scold

The old in love for fear
The god of love might hear

And hearing me might freeze
My five extremities.

Going to the Funeral

Death hushes all   the bigwigs   the big shots
the top brass   the bashaws   the bullet-proof
bosses   the shoguns   in long black dreadnaughts
come purring   the magnates   shipping   oil
the magnificoes   Oh my God   the unimpeachables
the homburgs   the silk hats   the sucked cigars
death hushes   death hushes   the czars   the nabobs
and still they come purring   the moguls   the mugwumps
the high-muck-a-mucks   Oh my God   Oh my God!

Four

Prescription

Whoever would be clean
Of cluttering desire
Must scrap the golden mean
And bed with frost or fire.

Only two ways to cure
The old itching disease:
No middle temperature
But only burn or freeze.

Water Poem

Waterflowers have no need to fear
The waterfowler since waterflowers
And fowlers live in different watery worlds.

Only waterfowl have a need to fear
The waterfowler whereas waterflowers
Only need to fear the fouling of waters.

Waterfowlers need a stamp to shoot
At waterfowl but waterflowers need
No stamp to shoot, no stamp at all at all.

Though a Fool

The wayfaring man though a fool
Will often fare as well
As one who has been to school
And knows how to scan and spell.

The scholar is melancholy
Too often on his way
While the fool may well be jolly
Though why he cannot say.

Three Ships

Oh for three ships, three gallant ships
On Christmas day
And every day in the morning.

Not battleship   marksmanship   brinkmanship
On Christmas day
Or any day in the morning.

But kinship   friendship   fellowship
On Christmas day
And every day in the morning.

Exemplary

They never ask for more
Or ever lose their poise
Never a slammed door
Never a needless noise.

For slander a deaf ear
So faultlessly well bred
Gossip they seldom hear
The deferential dead.

(Two Poems)

Stainless and steel
steeled against stain
where is the public man
year after year
unstainable
clean in his hardness
still public and still man?

Do not bend
do not bend the knee
to Baal
to Moluch
to the Pentagon
do not fold
do not fold the hands.

Five

Suspension

Where bees bowing from flower to flower
In their deliberation
Pause

And then resume—wherever bees
Cruising from goldenrod
To rose

Prolong the noon the afternoon
Fanning with wings of spun
Bronze

Sweetness on the unruffled air
Calore and *colore*
Where bees

The Bells: Italy

What are they saying that must be said
over and over?

As if the hills could not be trusted
a silent language?

Why so great certainty age on age,
hour after hour?

Or is it a question they keep asking
no one can answer?

Bouquets

One flower at a time, please
however small the face.

Two flowers are one flower
too many, a distraction.

Three flowers in a vase begin
to be a little noisy

Like cocktail conversation,
everybody talking.

A crowd of flowers is a crowd
of flatterers (forgive me).

One flower at a time. I want
to hear what it is saying.

Chrysanthemums

Your opulence in the fading year
Your daring, coming so late, an almost
Winter flower.

Your name is gold but you yourself
Bronze rather or snow or lemon.
Still you are golden.

Fountain of petals caught unfalling
Why are you not offspring of August
Riches to riches?

Three Old Ladies and
Three Spring Bulbs

I wouldn't be buried in anything but black
silk said Anne over her teacup
as the December afternoon dimmed to dusk.

I wouldn't be buried in anything but a white-
satin-and-ermine-lined incorruptible cypress
casket said Bertha over her stock quotations.

I wouldn't be buried in anything at all
said Clare at the open window my ashes
will sift as light as pear petals or snowflakes.

But Crocus, Hyacinth, and Tulip
brooding in autumn leaf-fall said I wouldn't
be buried in anything but good black earth.

Snowspell

Look, it is falling a little
faster than falling, hurrying
straight down on urgent business
for snowbirds, snowballs, glaciers.

It is covering up the afternoon.
It is bringing the evening down
on top of us and soon the night.
It is falling fast as rain.

It is bringing shadows wide
as eagles' wings and dark
as crows over our heads.
It is falling, falling fast.

Boy at a Certain Age

Perfectly rounded yet how slender
Supple, pliable, puppy-limber
Whole body lifts to lift a finger.

A mouth efficient for drinking, eating
Just as sufficient for shouting, beeping
But not yet for connected speaking.

A voice combining bass and treble
A mind more dreamable than thinkable
From chin to toe smooth as a pebble.

The Half Twist

What the camera did
To what the diver was doing

Alone by the lamp I
Contemplate I watch

What the camera did
To what the diver was doing

Not bird quite
And not quite human

What the camera did
To what the diver was doing.

The House Remembers

Faces, voices, yes of course
and the food eaten and the fires kindled
but the house also remembers feet.

Especially how one big pair used to pad
about comfortable as a cat's
bare on the bare wood floor.

And somebody else in clean white heavy socks
(his boots left at the door) would curl up
tailor-wise, Buddha-wise, on the couch

And only then the talk could really begin
and go on without end while listener
sat opposite and listened.

And once when one big toe had broken bounds
how someone took the sock and darned it
while the wearer sat and wondered.

Blisters to operate on but before
the sterile needle the basin of warm water
and someone kneeling as in the Last Supper.

What fireplace naturally remembers
are the cold feet it warmed but does it
recall the time when fire was not enough

And someone took bare feet in his bare hands
and chafed and cheered the blood
while the fire went on quietly burning?

When I Come

Once more the old year peters out—
all brightness is remembered
brightness.

> *(When I come, Bob,*
> *it won't be while just on my way*
> *to going somewhere else.)*

A small pine bough with nothing
better to do fingers
a windowpane.

> *(When I come, Bob—)*

Against the wet black glass a single
oval leaf fixed
like a face.

His Running My Running

Mid-autumn late autumn
At dayfall in leaf-fall
A runner comes running.

How easy his striding
How light his footfall
His bare legs gleaming.

Alone he emerges
Emerges and passes
Alone, sufficient.

When autumn was early
Two runners came running
Striding together

Shoulder to shoulder
Pacing each other
A perfect pairing.

Out of leaves falling
Over leaves fallen
A runner comes running

Aware of no watcher
His loneness my loneness
His running my running.

Retrospect

Yes, I was one of them. And what a cast
Of characters we were, a medley, hodgepodge,
No two with the same tongue, same skin, same god.
You would have guessed a carnival was coming,
Itinerant bazaar. Bazaar? Bizarre!

And the gifts, those blessed gifts, the gold for instance,
What a fine sample of irrelevance!
For if the child had actually been royal
He would have had more gold already than all
Our camels could bear. But if he was in fact
What all the evidence of our eyes declared
He was, a peasant baby, why then our gold
Was for the first robber who came along.
Or barring that, say the poor father tried
To buy a blanket for the kid, a warm
Blanket, picture the shopkeeper and his sneer:
Aha! just how did you come into *this?*

As for the frankincense, it would have taken
More than a ton of it to quell the reek
In that cowbarn. Yet I must say the steaming
Dung (and watch your step) and the cows themselves

Their warm flanks, their inoffensive breath
Made that cold spot appreciably less chilly.

I said I was one of them. Let me take that back.
If I was one of them or one *with* them
In going, I wasn't when we left for home—
Our separate and strangely scattered homes.
They had more faith than I. That is the way
They saw it. I, I was less credulous.
They found what they set out to find, believed
What they were ready, were programmed, to believe.
Do I sound superior? I don't mean to be.
I know as well as the next man that faith,
Some measure of faith, is needed by us all.
Pure doubt is death.
                    It was a long journey,
Long both in going and long in the return.
Tell me, why do we travel? Is it to find
What no one anywhere will ever find?
Or is it rather to find what we could just
As well have found at home? Travel? Travail.

Of course, to say the child was not a prince
Is not to say he may not, somehow, sometime,
Rise from his class, conceivably become
A peasant leader, a rebel, yes, a name.
Such things are not unknown. Or let us say
Someday a poet. There have been instances.
Who knows? A holy man? Yes, even a prophet?

Oh no, I don't rule out the chance our journey
—In spite of all I've said—still may have been
A little better than mistaken.